School Trouble

Lisa Bruce

Illustrated by
Lesley Harker

ORCHARD BOOKS

DYNAMITE DEELA

CONTENTS

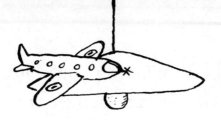

Chapter One

The table gave a little wobble. On top of the table, the chair gave a little wobble. On top of the chair, Deela wobbled.

Still, Deela stretched just that little bit higher. She almost had it. Her fingers touched the wing of her super stunter. It had glided to a halt on top of the light.

"You can do it, Deela," called her friends, encouragingly.

Yes, she could do it, just a little bit further and…

The bell for the end of playtime clanged. The classroom door swung open and their teacher, Mr Smith, strode in.

"DEELA! What do you think you are doing? Get down from there at once!"

Deela scrambled down, the super stunter held triumphantly in her hand.

"I will take that," Mr Smith plucked it from her grasp and put it away in his desk. "That was very dangerous, Deela." He glared around the room. "I don't want to catch anyone doing anything like that again."

Heads nodded.

"All right everybody, time to sit down."

Children scurried to their places with much clattering and scraping of chair legs.

"Quiet please…Jordan, stop picking your nose…Deela, pick up those books and next time LOOK where you are going."

The class settled down, except for Deela who finished straightening the fallen books.

"This afternoon," said Mr Smith, "we are

going to talk about something special."

The class held their breath excitedly wondering what was coming next.

"OK class, what do you know about Divali?"

The class looked a little crestfallen, this sounded like work, not a 'special'. Nobody put their hand up.

"Come on class, someone must know something. What about you, Deela?"

Deela had been so busy putting the books back that she hadn't been listening. She jumped when she heard her name.

"Sorry, Sir."

"Divali, Deela. What is it?"

"It's the festival of light, Sir."

"Good," said Mr Smith. "Now then, at Divali the tale of Rama and Sita is told and this term we are going to put on a Divali play."

"Yeah!"

"Brilliant, Sir!"

"Quiet everyone." Mr Smith held up his hand. "Now then, Mrs Cash from the Educational Charities Foundation will be visiting our school and I want to make a good impression on her. We may get a grant to build a swimming pool IF she thinks that we are a suitable school."

"A SWIMMING POOL!" The class went wild with delight.

"I only said 'if'. It all depends on you lot and how you behave, so let's start practising some quiet, shall we?"

Instantly the classroom was so silent that you could have heard a pencil being sharpened.

"Right," said Mr Smith. "Now let's listen to the story of Rama and Sita. Deela, have you finished? Good, could you bring me that book over there, please."

He pointed at the pile. The book that Mr Smith wanted was right at the bottom. It was a big book and a stubborn one. It wouldn't come out. Deela had to tug really hard and…whoops! The whole lot came crashing down again.

"Deela!" cried Mr Smith. "What are you doing?"

"Sorry, Sir."

Deela and her friend William walked home chattering excitedly. The news about the play was thrilling. All the juniors were going to be involved either acting or painting scenery or making costumes. Mr Smith had read them the story and Deela was especially pleased that there were lots of action scenes.

"I want to be the Monkey God!" She whooped along the street dancing like an orang-utan. "Don't you think that I'd make a good monkey, William?"

William chased after Deela making chattering screeches that were so like a chimpanzee that passers-by turned to stare.

"You are good," acknowledged Deela. "Perhaps I should be Rama, what do you think, Will?"

"Huh."

"Then I'd do battle with the evil demon. Take that." Deela sliced the air in front of her with a karate chop. "And that."

Deela aimed her bag at a menacing lamp post which they happened to be passing. The bag swung around the concrete post and bashed William in the chest.

WHACK!

"Ooof…"

"Sorry, Wills."

Deela helped him to get up.

"You'll never get the part of Rama."

"Why not?" Deela was indignant.

"Because," said William. "For one thing you're not a boy."

Deela exploded. "SO WHAT! I can act. I can dress up like a boy. I can probably be a better boy than any of you lot."

William didn't like arguments but he stuck to his guns.

"Even so, they won't give you the part."

"WHY?" Deela was red in the face with fury. William was supposed to be her best friend. Why was he saying stupid things like this!

"Because you are not tall enough."

Deela quietened down and William explained. "Your sister Dipali is going to be Princess Sita, so who ever plays Rama has to be as tall as her or taller."

"That's not fair."

"Well, I heard Mr Smith saying that maybe Nick or Peter from the top class could do it, they're both pretty tall."

"Peter! He is only a bit taller than me and as for Nick Parker, he can't act for toffee. I'd be much better than either of them."

William shrugged.

Deela was so angry that she felt all hot and her head started to ache.

"Maybe you'll get one of the other parts," William tried to console her.

"I want to be Rama," said Deela firmly. "Mr Smith is wrong to choose Peter or Nick. I will tell him tomorrow. You'll see."

Chapter Two

In the end Deela didn't tell Mr Smith. She didn't get the part of Rama or any other part. What she did get was a bad headache, a sore throat and a streaming nose.

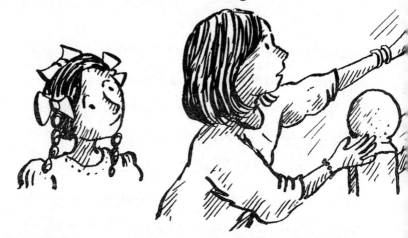

"Off to bed with you, Deela," her mother said the next morning when Deela couldn't face eating her breakfast.

"No, Mum. I've got to go to school."

"You're ill. You're not going anywhere."

Deela's mother was a nurse so she knew how to look after Deela. But she also expected her patients to do what they were told. Deela was packed back to bed still protesting and feeling very sorry for herself.

Deela missed the auditions and the selections. She was so ill that she was off school for the whole week.

By the time Deela was well enough to return, rehearsals were well underway. William was the monkey god, Nick Parker was the ten-headed demon, and Peter had the star part.

"What shall I do then, Mr Smith?" Deela asked dejectedly.

Mr Smith frowned and thought hard.

"Well," he said at long last. "We haven't got a prompt. You could do that."

"Does the prompt have lines to say?" Deela asked, a glimmer of hope in her eyes.

"No, you have to follow everybody else's lines."

"Do I get to go on stage though?" Deela was feeling desperate.

"Sorry, Deela. What you have to do is to sit here at the side and follow the script. If anybody freezes or forgets their lines you give them a prompt. OK?"

"OK," Deela nodded sadly. It was better than nothing she supposed.

As the rehearsals wore on Deela began to wish that she was doing something else. It was torment for her having to listen to people saying their lines atrociously or giggling and not paying attention.

Dipali was the worst. She thought that she was so good. She spent ages in front of the mirror, getting her hair 'just right.' Then she would glide onto the stage declaring her undying love for Rama (who always looked very embarrassed at that point) and fall into a dead faint when the wicked demon captured her.

"Dippy," said Deela one day. "Don't you think that Sita would fight back, you know, kick the demon in the shins or something?"

"Gracious me, of course not," Dipali retorted. "I might ruin my costume."

"Well, how about struggling a little bit?"

"I suppose I could," Dipali wiggled her shoulders slightly. "Like this, you mean?"

Deela sighed. Her sister hadn't really got a clue about acting, it was very frustrating.

William was funny. He did excellent monkey impressions at the beginning of all his lines.

"I will find Sita for you, Rama," he chittered. "If I have to search across the wide ocean."

"Now William, move to the back of the stage and look out across the sea," said Mr Smith. "Good. Now, wave that blue cloth at the back, girls. Make it look like the waving sea. What's the line here, Deela?"

"Only I can jump across the waters."

"When you say that William, I want you to leap off the stage."

"Yes, Sir."

William said his line and hopped off stage like a dancer with stomach ache.

"I can jump higher than that," said Deela to Mr Smith. "He looks as if he's playing hopscotch."

"Never mind. It will have to do."

Peter was worse. He charged about the stage brandishing his sword. In fact he got SO carried away in the battle scene that he always forgot his lines. Deela had to call them out to him so often that before long she was word perfect and didn't need to look at the book.

"Come out you wicked demon. I...er...I...?" Peter looked at Deela.

"I will cut off..." she prompted.

"Oh yes, I will cut off every one of your ten heads."

THWACK!

"OUCH! I'll get you for that, Peter."

"We're supposed to be fighting, numskull."

"If you want a fight, then I'll…"

"Oh yeah, pea-wit, what are you going to do?"

"Peter! Nick! Stop it, you two," Mr Smith shouted from the back of the hall.

"Listen, Peter," Mr Smith said patiently. "This is a play. It's pretend. You don't have to really hit Nick. Let's practise that bit again." He moved the demon army back into place. "And this time Rama, I want to be able to hear you from the back."

Peter went back to his position making a terrible face. He took a deep breath and opened his mouth wide.

"COME OUT YOU WICKED…"

Deela put her hands over her ears.

"Stop, STOP," called Mr Smith. "Peter, there's no need to shout, just speak clearly and loudly, you always seem to manage it in the playground. Let's try it again."

Deela sighed, every rehearsal was the same. Deela knew that she would have made a much better Rama than Peter, but how would she ever get the chance to prove it.

Chapter Three

The whole school was busy painting scenery, sewing costumes or making swords. A specially selected group from the top class were allowed to operate the lighting system and all those with acting parts learnt their lines.

On the way home from school Deela had taken to bounding across as many paving stones as she could manage.

"Come on froggie," she called back to William who was walking behind.

"I'm not a frog," he said.

"I know you're not," laughed Deela cheekily. "Because you can't jump."

"I can too."

"A flea can jump higher than you...even Dipali can jump higher than you. Once I told her there was a mouse under her chair. She jumped really high, then."

William went into a sulk.

Deela teased William about his jumping so much that he refused to do it any more.

Even Mr Smith couldn't persuade him to do any more than just stride off stage.

Then at one rehearsal Mr Smith produced a flying harness.

"I have hired it from a local theatre," he explained. "They use it for Peter Pan. Here, put this harness on, William."

William did as he was told and was attached to a long wire held securely on a pulley in the ceiling.

"When I pull on the other end you will be lifted up," Mr Smith flapped his arms. "Then you really will look as if you are making a gigantic leap. OK, William. Let's

try it."

William moved over to his position.

"Out of the way Peter!" Mr Smith yelled. "Right, after three jump up. One. Two. THREE."

William jumped and Mr Smith pulled on the other end of the wire. William dangled in the air before landing with a thud a few inches away.

"Not bad," said Mr Smith. "It will take some practise."

"Sir, can I have a go?"

"No, Peter. William is light, I can only just lift him."

"Oh, Sir…It looks brilliant. Pleease, Sir."

"I said NO, Peter."

"That's not fair."

Peter flounced away in a bad mood.

So, for the rest of the rehearsal Mr Smith practised making William jump in the air and by the end it really did look as if the monkey god was leaping across the sea. Peter was in a sulk. William's part was more exciting than his now. All he wanted was one little go.

Chapter Four

With only a week left to go before the first performance, the visitor arrived. Everyone had to be on their best behaviour.

Deela's class were putting the finishing touches to the forest scenery. Several large trees were spread over the table in front of them and Deela and her friends were busy painting them.

"Pass the green, would you."

Sophie, who was sitting beside Deela, jumped up and reached across the table for the green paint pot.

"Give that back," cried Lucy. "I haven't finished with it yet."

Sophie made a grab at Deela's paint pot but Deela saw her coming and whisked it out of the way. Sophie snatched again and this time managed to grab the pot. Paint slopped out all over Deela's uniform.

ex "Look what you've done!" she exclaimed.

Sophie said that she was sorry and ran to the sink to wet a paper towel. That only made the splodge blotchier.

"Mum will blame ME," said Deela.

Sophie sat down but only stayed still for a few seconds before jumping up to get the glue. This time she jogged Deela's arm just as she was painting an apple. The brush

shot across the page leaving a wide red trail.

"SOPHIE!" Deela shouted getting really annoyed. "Sit still will you."

Lucy sniggered.

"Sorry," Sophie apologised. "I'll paint over that, don't worry."

Quickly she reached for the green paint and nudged Deela's arm again.

Deela was fuming. Sophie was going to ruin her painting if she didn't stop leaping up and down.

Two minutes later when Sophie knocked the water over the table, Deela decided that enough was enough. She was going to MAKE Sophie sit still.

The next time Sophie jumped up, Deela picked up the pot of glue and spread it thickly all over the empty chair.

"Good," she thought replacing the brush in the pot. "At last we can get on."

Just then the classroom door opened and in came the Head followed by a lady in a posh cream suit.

"Good afternoon, Y4," the Head smiled. "This is Mrs Cash."

"Good-after-noon-Mrs-Cash," chanted Deela's class.

The Head spotted Sophie by the sink.

"Ah, Sophie, could you please run along to the staff room and give this key to whoever is in there."

Sophie left on her errand and Mrs Cash began to wander around the classroom looking at the work that the children were doing. She came over to Deela's desk.

"What are you doing here?" she asked politely.

Everyone was tongue-tied.

"Painting," said Deela at last. She wondered why Mrs Cash had needed to ask.

"How wonderful," Mrs Cash smiled through thick pink lipstick. "Can I watch?" She moved to the space next to Deela.

"Oh no!" Deela panicked.

"Actually, we've nearly finished," Deela said quickly.

"No we haven't," said Lucy puzzled. "There's all this side to do."

Before Deela could stop her Mrs Cash had pulled out Sophie's chair and planted her smart cream bottom on it. Deela felt a queasy churning in her stomach. This was not what she had meant to happen.

"I am looking forward to your play," said Mrs Cash. "What scene is this from?"

Deela couldn't think of anything except the glue.

"Are you all right?" Mrs Cash turned to Deela. "You don't look very well."

Deela swallowed, her throat was suddenly very dry.

"I'm very sorry," she whispered.

Mrs Cash looked concerned.

"What do you mean?" She felt Deela's forehead. "You feel all hot, dear. Here, let me get you a glass of water…"

Then she discovered what Deela was talking about.

The telling off that Deela got from the Head was the worst that she had EVER had. Did she realise what a senseless thing she had done? Did she know how much the school was going to have to pay to have Mrs Cash's suit cleaned? If the school didn't get the money for the swimming pool now, it was all HER fault…

Deela felt ashamed.

"And," finished the Head, "you can stay in at lunch time and clean all the glue off Sophie's chair."

Not only did the visit get off to a bad start, it got worse. And guess whose fault it was…!

It all happened on the day of the play. Deela's class were putting the final touches to a collage for the wall. William and Sophie were helping Mr Smith to stick their poems and stories on the wall whilst Deela and the others cut out shapes.

"Any more small flames ready yet?" called Mr Smith. "I want to put a group of them up at the top here."

"Here you are, Sir."

"Thanks, William." Mr Smith took the shapes and climbed the ladder. He began positioning the flames in a pattern of clusters that looked like fires.

"Hey, move over will you, Deela."

"Yes, look how much space you are taking up."

Deela was doing a beautiful lamp shape to go under her flame but the others on the table kept elbowing her so she carefully placed the gold coloured paper on her lap and carried on.

"You should have heard Peter the other day, he thinks that the story should be rewritten so that Rama makes the big jump," Sophie said.

"That's silly," Deela laughed.

"It's only because he wants to fly on the rope thing."

"Hurry up with those scissors, Deela."

Deela chewed her lip, concentrating hard on her cutting out. It was a beautiful lamp.

"Come on, Deela."

"All right, all right, I've nearly finished."

Deela snipped the last snip. Satisfied, she held up a perfect lamp shape in shiny gold paper...and one in navy blue material!

Deela looked down in horror and saw the hole in her skirt.

"Oh no!"

"Oh, Deela, what have you done now!" cried Mr Smith.

Deela was sent to the cloakroom to change into her PE shorts for the rest of the day. She wanted to finish her lamp so she took the short cut, across the Hall. It was eerie in the empty Hall so Deela ran across as fast as she could.

Just as Deela reached the door her knee caught in the hole of her ruined skirt, sending her sprawling forwards in a frenzied lurch. Automatically she put her hands up to the door to break her fall.

This would have been all right if the Head hadn't chosen exactly that moment to open it. Deela pitched straight into the arms of…Mrs Cash, carrying a large armful of files.

Papers swooshed in the air like snow white fireworks and floated gently down to the floor in any order they felt like. Deela and the lady sat on the floor, winded, staring at each other.

"YOU, again!"

"I'm terribly sorry," Deela apologised. "It was an accident."

"Deela," the Head was REALLY angry this time. "What were you doing?"

"I'm sorry…I…I…fell."

She showed them the lamp shape in her skirt, which now had a long tear from one corner all the way down to the hem.

"Deela, you must be the only person that I know who can trip over something which isn't there!" sighed the Head. "Go and get changed and this time DON'T RUN."

Deela turned and meekly left the hall.

"Here, let me help you with these." The Head bent down and picked up some of the papers. "I don't know what to do with that girl. She means well but she is always getting into trouble!"

"Thanks," Mrs Cash took the papers from the Head and straightened her pile. "Well, if you will just show me where the back files are kept I will get on."

"Certainly. I'm afraid that it's a bit gloomy under the stage but there is enough space to stand up."

The Head lifted up a trap door in the middle of the stage and was about to go down when the school secretary popped her head around the door.

"Excuse me, but there's a phone call for you. I think it's one of the Governors."

The Head hesitated for a moment.

"Don't worry about me," said Mrs Cash taking the torch. "I'll just have a quick look at a few things down here, then I'm finished. You go and take your call and I'll see you at the play this afternoon."

When Deela came back into the hall dressed in her PE shorts, she found it empty again. This time though she was very careful when she opened the door.

'That's odd,' thought Deela seeing the wide open trap door. 'We're not using the trap door in this play.'

Cautiously Deela approached the hole and peered in. It looked very dark.

"Hello," called Deela. "Is anybody there?"

It was unlucky that at the moment Mrs

Cash answered, the bell rang for lunch time. Apart from the bell Deela didn't hear a thing.

"I'd better close this," thought Deela. "It's very dangerous, somebody could fall in and have an accident."

Hearing the stampede in the corridor, Deela shut the trap door and ran off to join the midday rush for the dining room.

Chapter Five

That afternoon, it was bedlam on the stage as children rushed excitedly around in magnificent costumes, checking that their props were in place or practising their lines for the last time. Mr Smith went through the final checks.

"Where is Sita's jewellery?"

"Dipali, you look great."

"Sir, Peter is hitting me."

"Stop it, Peter."

"Mind out of the way, please."

"What's that noise?"

"I don't know."

"Maybe it's your knees knocking with nerves, Dippy."

"Got your script, Deela?"

"Yes, but I don't need it."

"Peter, leave that rope alone."

"Are you sure that you can't hear a noise?"

"STOP FIGHTING, PETER!"

"You know, I'm sure that I can hear something."

Then Mr Smith called everybody together on the stage for a final briefing. On the other side of the curtain came the muffled sounds of the first parents arriving.

"OK everybody, quiet please."

A charged hush fell over the children. This was their big moment.

"You have all worked extremely hard for…"

KNOCK! KNOCK!

"Sir, there's that noise again."

"I know Dipali, it must be someone in the audience. Now, as I was saying…"

KNOCK! KNOCK! KNOCK!

"I don't think that it is coming from the audience," said Dipali looking worried. "It's coming from…under my feet!"

Mr Smith went over to where Dipali and Deela were and listened. Sure enough, there it was again. A faint tapping sound.

"It's coming from the trap door," said Deela helpfully. "Oh no! The trap door…"

Mr Smith undid the bolt and lifted the door. Out of the gloom staggered a figure, covered in dust and cobwebs.

"How did YOU get down there?" he asked innocently.

"Somebody," Mrs Cash snarled through clenched teeth. "Somebody locked me in there this morning." Her eyes roamed over the crowd of children and fixed on Deela. "YOU," she said pointing her painted fingernail accusingly, "it was you, wasn't it?"

"I'm sorry. I didn't know you were there."

Mrs Cash stepped towards her, a look of anger in her eyes.

Fortunately Mr Smith took charge of the situation. He behaved as if having an important visitor locked up under the stage just before a school play was a perfectly normal event in his day. He stepped out in front of Mrs Cash.

"You sit down right here," he said leading her to a chair. "Sophie and Dipali go to the staff room and fetch a glass of water." He looked at his watch. "Hurry, there's only four minutes before the curtain goes up. Deela go and sit down, I don't want any more trouble from you."

On the other side of the curtain the school choir began singing the music that signalled the start of the performance and the last of the parents settled into their seats.

"Do you want to go and watch from the front?" Mr Smith asked Mrs Cash.

"I do not," she replied haughtily. "Just look at the state of me, I'm covered with filth." She paused to brush some dust off her blouse. "No, I will watch from here."

There is a saying 'the show must go on' and that is exactly what happened. The curtain rose on the scene of Rama and Sita's wedding. Dipali declared her love for Rama and as usual Peter got embarrassed and forgot his lines. Rama and Sita were then expelled from the kingdom by his wicked step-mother.

Back stage Mrs Cash calmed down. She got up and stood by the side to watch the action on the stage.

All went well until half way through when it came to the Monkey God's jump over the ocean. William was clipped to the wire. Mr Smith stood ready to heave on the other end and William spoke.

"Only I can jump across the waters," he said proudly to Rama as he ran into his jump.

Mr Smith pulled with all his might. William's feet left the floor and Peter leapt onto William. This was the only chance that he would get to have a go at flying and nobody could tell him off until afterwards. Peter was delighted.

Mr Smith was taken by surprise by the sudden extra weight. He staggered and almost let go of the rope. William and Peter swung dangerously and lurched offstage.

From her chair at the side, Deela saw everything. She also saw that the two were swinging off course. They were swinging directly towards...Mrs Cash, who had no idea that anything was wrong.

There was no time to think. Deela did the only thing possible. Screaming a warning she jumped out of her seat and ran. With her head down like a charging bull Deela smashed into Mrs Cash sending her hurtling to the ground. The flying pair came crashing to the ground seconds later, landing on the spot where the lady had been standing.

The audience clapped loudly at the special effect and the monkey army gathered to wait for Rama's next line.

Behind the scenes there was chaos.

"Are you all right?" Deela said getting up off Mrs Cash, who was winded but otherwise unhurt.

"Yes, I am," she replied dusting herself down AGAIN. "Thank you. I would have been hurt by those two."

Peter, meanwhile, was paying for his stupidity. He had landed badly and was now crying with the sharp pain in his ankle. On stage, the monkeys waited and waited, not knowing what to do. The audience began to titter, realising that there was something wrong. What was going to happen without Rama?

The monkey army stood nervously watching the spot that Rama should have been in, hoping for a miracle.

"Monkeys, your leader has done well to bring me news of my beloved Sita."

The monkey army looked surprised, for Rama was back, but shorter than before and dressed in a school sweatshirt and PE shorts! Deela had taken over.

She was the only one who knew the part. The monkeys smiled and gave their cheer.

"Now," said Rama. "We must work out how to cross this mighty ocean ourselves…"

The show went on.

After the final curtain had been drawn Mrs Cash came up to Deela.

"You were marvellous," she said smiling. "The whole thing was nearly a disaster, but you saved the day. Congratulations."

Deela grinned from ear to ear. All her class crowded round her.

"You're a star, Deela!"

Here are some other Orchard books you might enjoy ...

FIZZY HITS THE HEADLINES

1 85213 485 2 (hbk)   1 85213 518 2 (pbk)

FIZZY STEALS THE SHOW

1 85213 785 1 (hbk)   1 85213 823 8 (pbk)

FIZZY TV STAR

1 85213 996 X (hbk)   1 86039 234 2 (pbk)

BEN'S BEAN

1 85213 825 4 (hbk)   1 85213 820 3 (pbk)

THE LOLLIPOP WITCH

1 85213 728 2 (hbk)   1 85213 849 1 (pbk)

AMY AND THE WEATHER WIZARD

1 85213 881 5 (hbk)   1 86039 075 7 (pbk)